MARVEL
SPIDER-MAN
DARK WEBS

© 2020 MARVEL

AUTUMN
PUBLISHING

Spidey was on his way to meet Miles Morales and Gwen Stacy for a training session.

"Hey!" an old woman shouted. "There's a goo monster down there, Spider-Kid. Get it out!"

"The name is actually Spider-Man," he said. "And that thing you're smelling? It isn't a goo monster. That's just our wonderfully stinky city."

"Thanks for being a concerned citizen, though," Spider-Man said, firing his web-shooters and taking off in a flash. "Have a nice day, okay?"

After changing out of his suit, Peter Parker joined Gwen and Miles at the Midtown High science lab.

"Hey, pals. What have we got?" he asked, cheerfully.

Peter noticed the curious device Gwen was tinkering with. "What's that thing?" he asked.

"Just a sound cannon Miles is helping me work on," Gwen said. "I'm putting the final touches on the battery pack now."

"Awesome! But we better get going," Peter said.

"Today we're going to go through a couple of simple training exercises," Spider-Man said a few minutes later, once they'd got to the roof and changed into their suits. "Make sure to pay attention. You've got to work hard if you want to be a Super Hero."

Spider-Man put Miles and Gwen through their paces with lots of different exercises!

Then, the heroes put on their masks. "Enough exercise. I want to show you guys something. I've been working on my bio-electric venom blasts. They can mess up all kinds of technology," Miles said.

"Oh yeah? Throw a few of them my way," said Spider-Man.

FZZZT! FZZZT! FZZZT! Spider-Man flipped through the air doing acrobatic tricks to avoid Miles.

"Your venom blasts are too wild and uncontrolled. You're not focusing on your target," Spider-Man called down. "Guess you need more training than I originally thought."

Gwen rolled her eyes. "Know-it-all," she muttered.

Then, Gwen had a very odd feeling.
"Guys, my spider-sense is tingling really bad,"
she said.

On the street below, long black tendrils suddenly appeared out of the sewers and began throwing unsuspecting citizens into the air.

"Uh-oh," Miles said. He spun a web that caught the citizens before they hit the ground. "That was close."

"What's happening, Spidey?" asked Gwen.

A burly black creature emerged from the spiralling tendrils.
"Venom," growled Spider-Man.

Gwen knew the name well. "The alien that bonded itself to a human host named Eddie Brock!" she exclaimed.

"You don't really want to hurt people, Eddie!" Spider-Man called out.

"EDDIE CAN'T HEAR YOU, SSSSSSPIDER-MAN,"
the villain hissed. "There's only Venom now."

"Well, looks like it's spider-time!" cheered Spider-Man.
"That's a new catchphrase I'm testing out. Like it?
The other option was 'time to get your spider on!'"

Venom's tendrils inched closer to Spider-Man's feet.

Spider-Man flung himself away from Venom's creeping tendrils. "Gwen, you make sure the civilians are safe," he ordered. "Miles, it might be time to put those bio-electric blasts to work."

Venom swung his tendrils in all directions, smashing everything in sight. Miles aimed his blasts at the Super Villain.

SMASH! Gwen hurried to stop a piece of debris from falling onto a small group of tourists. "Welcome to New York City," she said, straining. "Sorry about the mess."

"And now your friendly neighbourhood web-head swings in for the grand finale," Spider-Man said.

THWIP! He shot sticky webbing in Venom's face. "My newest batch of webbing is stronger than ever," Spidey called to his friends. But...

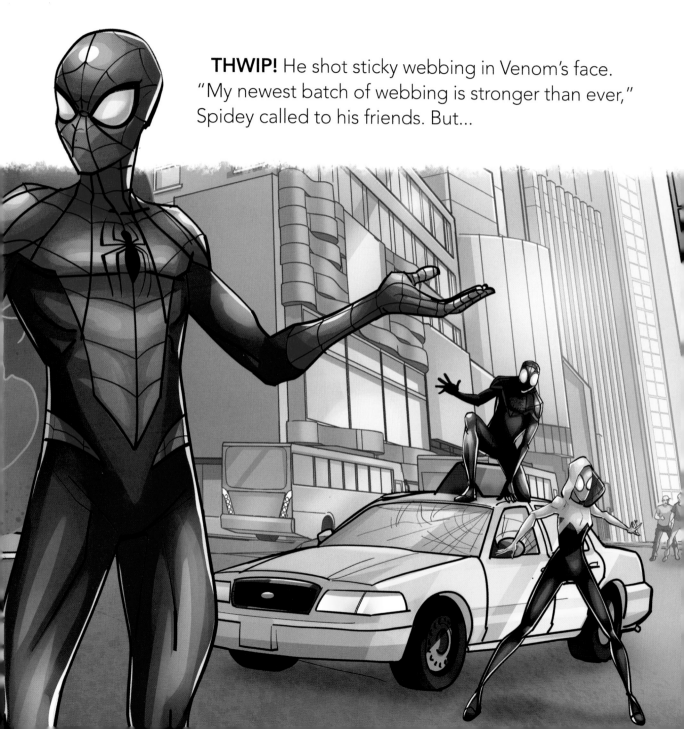

... **SWACK!** Venom knocked Spider-Man out cold.

"WHO'S NEXT?" Venom sneered. Miles and Gwen pulled Spidey to safety.

"I think I know how to take him down for good," Gwen said to Miles. "But I'll need you to keep him distracted for a couple of minutes."

Miles spotted a brightly lit marquee hanging above Venom.
Perfect, he thought.

"BAM!" Miles shouted. He fired off a round of venom blasts at the
marquee, causing a shower of sparks to rain down on Venom.

"Nice work. Be right back!" Gwen said, swinging away.

Gwen arrived at Midtown High to retrieve her sound cannon.
Gwen strapped on the harness and grabbed the battery pack, checking
it one more time before putting it in place.

"I sure hope this works!" Gwen returned to Miles and a still-knocked-out Spider-Man, ready to end the battle once and for all. "Plug your ears," she said. "I'm about to turn things up."

Gwen unleashed the full power of the sound cannon on Venom as he struggled to preserve his monstrous form. "Sssssstop!" he screeched. "Make it ssssssstop!"

"Keep going!" exclaimed Miles. Soon, Venom's body reverted to a puddle of goo, revealing Eddie Brock's human form underneath.

The police rushed onto the scene and took Eddie to jail. Gwen was relieved that the sound cannon worked!

Even in his confused state, Spider-Man felt bad that he hadn't thought his friends were ready to help him fight crime. "I was wrong earlier when I said all you've got to do is work hard," said Spider-Man.

"A real hero also needs to work smart, like both of you did, especially if they're going to wear a spider on their chest." He paused. "I'm glad we're a team."

"I told you so, Spider-Kid!"
the old lady cried, suddenly
reappearing. "It was a goo monster
all along!"

"Ummmm. Who's that?" asked Miles.

Spidey cringed. "Ah, just one of my fans.
Okay then, off we go!"

Miles cheered as the trio swung into the sky.
"IT'S SPIDER-TIME!"

Gwen smiled. "I like the sound of that."